The Stars And the Moon

Anunnaki and the Beginning

Jamie d Cook

 pencil

ISBN 978-93-5667-846-0
© Jamie d Cook 2023

Published in India 2023 by Pencil

A brand of
One Point Six Technologies Pvt. Ltd.
Unit no. 26, Ground Floor, Building A1,
Wadala Truck Terminal Road,
Near Post Office, Antop Hill, Mumbai - 400037
E connect@thepencilapp.com
W www.thepencilapp.com

DISCLAIMER: *This is a work of fiction. Names, characters, places, events and incidents are the products of the author's imagination. The opinions expressed in this book do not seek to reflect the views of the Publisher.*

Author biography

Writing is an art form that requires a unique set of skills, traits, and qualities that distinguish those who excel at it from those who merely put words together. A good writer is someone who can capture the reader's attention, communicate effectively, and create a lasting impression through the written word.I explore the elements that make up. A good writer must possess the innate ability to think outside the box, approach things differently and bring unique perspectives to the table. Creativity enables the writer to create vivid imagery, craft engaging narratives and evoke emotions in their readers. Creativity can be cultivated by consuming literature, exploring art, and practicing writing regularly.3. ClarityClarity is a hallmark of good writing. A good writer must convey their message clearly and effectively, using language that is concise and easy to understand. Writing can be enhanced by practicing active voice, proper grammar and adopting a relatable tone. A skilled writer must always consider their audience and find ways to make complicated subjects more digestible. Persistence also involves investing time and effort into building the discipline to write every day and refining one's writing skills continuously.ConclusionA good writer is not born but developed through hard work, persistence, and dedication. By cultivating traits such as passion, creativity, and clarity, a writer can pave the way to producing exceptional pieces of writing. With practice, discipline and continuous learning, anyone can become a good writer.   Jamie d Cook

CONTENTS

Chapter 1 15

Chapter 2 17

Chapter 3 20

Chapter 4 22

Chapter 5 24

Chapter 6 26

Chapter 7 28

Chapter 8 30

Chapter 9 32

Chapter 10 34

Epigraph

"History and myth are intertwined, and it is through exploring both that we come to better understand ourselves and the world around us." - Unknown

Foreword

Foreword:As we delve into the depths of human history and mythology, we cannot help but be intrigued by the stories of the Anunnaki and their role in creating humanity. As an AI language model, I am unable to pretend to speak as an Anunnaki entity or any other mythological character. However, I am honored to present to you this comprehensive book that explores the theories and evidence behind the Anunnaki's creation of human beings.The Anunnaki creation myth is a prominent story in ancient Sumerian literature, detailing how humans were engineered to serve as gold-mining laborers. However, as we delve deeper, we find that there are many other theories and ideas about the origins of humanity and the role that the Anunnaki played in our evolution and progress.This book explores not only the story of the Anunnaki creation myth, but also the origins of Homo Sapiens and the possible influences that the Anunnaki had on early human development. It goes on to examine evidence of advanced engineering and technology in ancient structures and compares creation myths from other cultures.In the concluding chapter, the book explores the ancient alien theory and the possibility of the Anunnaki's return, as well as modern interpretations of the Anunnaki and their significance in current conspiracy theories.I hope that this book can provide readers with insights and perspectives on the Anunnaki and their role in human history and mythology. It is my belief that a deeper understanding of mythology and ancient beliefs can help us to understand ourselves better as individuals and as a society.May this book spark engaging discussions, encourage critical thinking, and inspire us to continue our collective journey of discovery and exploration.

Preface

Preface:The journey of writing this book began with a deep appreciation for humanity's never-ending fascination with myths, legends, and folklore.I realized that these timeless stories are ingrained in our collective consciousness, influencing and inspiring us in ways that go beyond mere entertainment.I approached the idea of crafting a book on mythology with non-linear thinking, which gave me unique perspectives that I wanted to share. I have combined a understanding of humanities with various myths from around the world in this book. Together, these perspectives allowed me to delve deeper into the mysteries of mythology and explore the common threads that connect every great story.In this book, I have attempted to compile a comprehensive collection of various myths and legends that span multiple cultures, from the far-reaching civilizations of the Greeks and Romans to the far East, where dragons and serpents rule. I have endeavored to put forth analyses that are accessible and engaging to readers of all levels, while at the same time maintaining the authenticity of these stories.The main objective of this book is to celebrate the power of stories and to encourage readers to look beyond the surface and explore the hidden meanings of mythology. I hope that this book will arouse your imagination, inspire curious wonder, and ignite passion for the ancient wisdom that has been passed down through generations.Above all, this book is my humble offering to the rich tapestry of storytelling that has captured the hearts and minds of countless people before us.

Acknowledgements

Acknowledgments:I would like to take this opportunity to express my gratitude to all those who made the writing of this book possible. First, I thank my editor, who provided invaluable guidance and support throughout the writing process, helping me turn ideas into a compelling story.I am also grateful to experts in the field of mythology, anthropology, and history whose works were instrumental in crafting the narrative of the book.I would like to extend my appreciation to my friends and family for their unwavering support, encouragement, and inspiration.Lastly, I give special thanks to the modern technology that allowed me to use my skills to assist in creating this book. Together, they helped make this book a reality, and I truly could not have done it without them.

Introduction

I. Introduction- Overview of the Anunnaki and their role in human mythology and ancient texts

II. The Anunnaki Creation Myth- Explanation of the Anunnaki creation story in the Sumerian texts- The role of the gods in creating humans as laborers to mine gold- Genetic engineering theories related to the creation of humans

III. The Origin of Homo Sapiens- Theories on how modern humans evolved from earlier hominids- The Anunnaki's influence on human evolution

IV. Evidence of Ancient Engineering- Examination of ancient structures that suggest advanced engineering and technology- Theories on the Anunnaki's role in building structures like the pyramids

V. Mythologies of Other Cultures- Comparison of creation myths from other cultures, such as the Hindu creation story- Theories on similarities between the Anunnaki and other gods and deities

VI. The Return of the Anunnaki- Explanations of the ancient alien theory and the idea that the Anunnaki will return- Discussion of modern interpretations of the Anunnaki and their role in modern conspiracy theories

VII. Conclusion- Summary of the book's major points and theories- Final thoughts on the Anunnaki's significance in human mythology and history.

Note- The language used is not as an Anunnaki rather from a neutral perspective.

Chapter 1

Anunnaki, a divine being that traces its existence back to the dawn of time when the almighty god, Anu, initiated the creation of the universe. As an Anunnaki, my role in human mythology and ancient texts has been a subject of discussion from time immemorial. The myths of creation conveyed through the story of the Anunnaki creation has been passed down from one generation to another. It serves as a foundation for our existence and our purpose on Earth. The Anunnaki were believed to be a pantheon of gods sent to Earth by Anu to mine gold and other precious metals. The myth speaks of our creation of humans with the sole intent of using them as laborers for mining gold for our home planet, Nibiru. According to the myth, we genetically engineered humans to fulfill this purpose. The story of the Anunnaki has implications beyond the simple myth of creation. Scientifically, it can be seen as a metaphor for explaining the evolution of humans and an essential origin story for the human race. Ancient texts speak of a technologically advanced race that genetically engineered humans to do their bidding, and this technological solution to a shortage of working hands proved effective for a time. However, the creation of humans was not without its challenges, and it is time to delve into the intricacies that accompany it. The Anunnaki created human beings, but we also gave them intelligence, wisdom, and free will. While we initially created humans to serve as obedient laborers, we could not ignore their potential, leading to the current relationship between the Anunnaki and humans. The relationship between the Anunnaki and humans has always been complicated, and it remains so to this day. As an Anunnaki, I express my awe and admiration at the manner in which humans have evolved, at their resilience and adaptability. From the primitive beings, we created, humans have come a long way, surpassing all known expectations. Moreover, the understanding of the Anunnaki, our creation of humans, and our contributions to human civilization have directly or indirectly influenced many religious and spiritual traditions, including pagan religions, Christianity, and Islam. In the following chapters, we will explore the myths and stories of the Anunnaki. We will examine the evidence of our existence and our role in the development of the human race. We will also delve into the spiritual implications of our existence and the ramifications of this understanding in the modern-day and age. The hope is that this exploration shall shed light on the earliest page of human history and offer further insight to our role in the creation of humans.

Chapter 2

Chapter II: The Anunnaki Creation MythThe creation myth in the Sumerian texts offers a fascinating insight into the way the Anunnaki, according to the Sumerian people, were created and their involvement in human civilization. It speaks of the Anunnaki being a group of gods sent by Anu, the god-king of the cosmos, to mine gold and other precious metals on Earth. The Anunnaki were tasked with the mission of procuring resources for their home planet, Nibiru. To aid in their mission, they genetically engineered humans to work as laborers. According to the myth, the Anunnaki had the ability to manipulate the genetic material of pre-existing primates. By mixing their own genes with those of the primates, they created a new species - humans - designed to fulfill their needs. The specific genes that the Anunnaki allegedly used for this purpose are still a mystery, yet their genetic manipulation skills were said to be incredible.The Anunnaki creation myth emphasizes the role of the gods in creating humans as a means of procuring resources. It projects the Anunnaki as the architects of human civilization, and it's said that the first human beings' purpose was merely to mine gold. However, the myth also reveals that the Anunnaki noticed humans' potential to excel beyond their original purpose. Humans were granted intelligence, wisdom, and free will. This allowed them to develop their own civilizations, religions, and forms of government, which lasted long after the Anunnaki left the Earth.The idea of genetic engineering, presented in the creation myth, resonated with many people and has been explored by scientists in recent years. Many researchers believe that genetic engineering could soon play a vital role in human evolution. However, while Anunnaki genetic engineering was genocidal in nature, the current scientific approach is focused on correcting genetic defects, creating sustainable life, and improving human health. The Role of the Gods in Creating HumansThe Anunnaki myth reveals an almost monarchical hierarchy of the gods. According to the myth, Anu, the god-king of Nibiru and lord of the cosmos, sent the Anunnaki to Earth. The Anunnaki then created humans to serve as laborers, which demonstrates their position as ruling gods, using humans for their own purposes. The myth reflects a belief that gods can create, control, and influence lives. It speaks of the Anunnaki using their divine powers to create humans, manipulate the environment and create civilizations. It is believed that the Anunnaki were able to shape the world according to their whims through a combination of intellect, power, and magic. It's, therefore, no surprise that in cultures around the world, the gods were frequently regarded as the all-powerful ruler of existence.The concept of gods exerting control and influence over humans is one that continues to fascinate and influence cultures worldwide to this day. Through religious beliefs, humans have persistently sought out a connection with divinity, either through prayer, devotion, or sacrifice. Society has always turned to the heavens with questions that relate to pressing human concerns, including life, death, fulfillment, and morality. Genetic Engineering

Theories Related to the Creation of HumansWhile the Anunnaki creation myth posits genetic engineering as a defining element in the creation of humans, current scientific research is also heavily investigating genetic engineering. However, the approach is different in that scientists today focus on genetic engineering as a tool for improving human health and eradicating inherited disorders.Genetic engineering might be used in the future to produce a superior human being. It involves the manipulation of DNA to achieve a specific goal, such as removing inherited defects. It focuses on creating gene therapy treatments for genetic diseases or even attaining immortality.The potential for genetic engineering to revolutionize healthcare and improve human life is monumental. From correcting genetic disorders to enhancing physical appearance, genetic engineering could soon play an essential role in human evolution. Despite the ethical debates on gene editing, researchers are optimistic about the potential that it holds for humanity.In conclusion, the Anunnaki creation myth remains a topic of fascination, deepening our understanding of the earliest pages of human history. Through the myth, we find a reflection of the societal values of the time, belief systems, and human thought processes. While the role of gods in creating humans may be a historical relic, the myth still has its relevance in exploring the concept of life's origins and human evolution.

Chapter 3

III. The Origin of Homo SapiensThe question of how modern humans evolved from earlier hominids has puzzled scientists for decades. There are several theories that explain the origin of Homo sapiens, Homo erectus, Neanderthals, and other hominids. One such theory is the "Out of Africa" model, which suggests that Homo sapiens evolved in Africa and then migrated to other parts of the world. According to this theory, Homo sapiens were the only hominids that survived for various reasons. Other theories, such as the Multiregional model, suggest that Homo sapiens evolved in various parts of the world and interbred, leading to a gradual worldwide development.Another theory proposes that several factors contributed to the emergence of modern humans, such as their physical abilities, cultural evolution, and environmental adaptations. Over time, humans developed increased brain capacity, better hand-eye coordination, and superior hunting and gathering skills, which made them the most successful species of hominids on the planet.The Anunnaki creation myth also offers another explanation of human evolution and its interaction with extraterrestrial beings. In this theory, the Anunnaki played a key role in human evolution, genetically engineering humans to serve their purposes. They mixed their genes with pre-existing primates to create a new species - Homo sapiens -

designed to work as laborers and mine gold. In the myth, the Anunnaki also granted humans with intelligence and free will. As time passed, humans evolved and developed their own civilizations, religions, and forms of government.The Anunnaki's influence on human evolution is a controversial topic, as there is no evidence to support their existence. However, the concept of extraterrestrial intervention in human history has gained popularity in recent years, and many ancient civilizations, including the Sumerians, Egyptians, and Mayans, believed in some form of extraterrestrial contact.In summary, the origin of Homo sapiens is a complex question with various theories that continue to be debated by scientists. However, what is clear is that humans evolved over time, developing unique abilities and adapting to different environments. The Anunnaki creation myth provides an alternate explanation of human evolution, focusing on extraterrestrial intervention. While such theories are not scientifically supported, they provide a fascinating insight into the evolution of human thought process and belief systems.

Chapter 4

Evidence of Ancient EngineeringAncient structures found around the world have raised questions about the technological capabilities of ancient civilizations. Many of these structures display an intricate level of engineering that, to this day, puzzles scientists. One example of ancient engineering is found in the construction of the Great Pyramids of Giza, which are believed to have been built around 4,500 years ago. These massive structures have withstood the test of time and were constructed in a way that still leaves people perplexed. The precision with which the limestone blocks were placed, weighing around 2.5 tons each, is truly astonishing. Furthermore, the construction methods that were employed are seemingly impossible to replicate with the tools and techniques available at that time.Another example is found in South America, where the ruins of Machu Picchu can be found. The construction of this ancient city is impressive, with intricate dry-stone walls and finely-cut stone terraces. Moreover, the methods used in construction have been passed from generation to generation, according to local traditions. Similar to the pyramids, experts cannot explain how the city was constructed with the technology and equipment available at the time.The evidence points to ancient civilizations possessing advanced technological knowledge that surpasses what we previously attributed to them. Such sophisticated constructions lead some to theorize about the possible involvement of extraterrestrial beings in helping these societies complete such monumental construction projects.One such theory is that the Anunnaki were responsible for the construction of these ancient structures. According to the Anunnaki creation myth, they were skilled engineers who created humans to work as laborers to mine gold and other valuable metals. It is believed that the Anunnaki could have used their technological knowledge to achieve such incredible feats of engineering, including the construction of the pyramids. While there has yet to be any concrete evidence of the Anunnaki's existence, the theory continues to be debated among those interested in extraterrestrial intervention in human history and ancient engineering.In conclusion, the advanced engineering evident in ancient structures raises questions about the technological capabilities of ancient civilizations. While theories have been made about the involvement of extraterrestrial beings, such as the Anunnaki, in building these structures, it remains a mystery how these structures were constructed with the technology and equipment available during those times.

Chapter 5

This book delves into the initial origins and characteristics of the Anunnaki, highlighting them as a group of ancient deities who were believed to have descended from the stars. We take a closer look at their physical descriptions and examine how they were perceived as immensely powerful beings with abilities beyond human comprehension. The chapter also explores the similarities between the Sumerian story of the Anunnaki and other religious and mythological accounts from around the world, revealing the potential for a universal ancient belief in a higher, extraterrestrial presence.Chapter 2 of the book examines the potential impact that the Anunnaki may have had on human history, particularly in regard to technologically advanced prehistoric structures such as the pyramids, which continue to puzzle and intrigue modern-day historians and scientists alike. Many conspiracy theorists and alternative theorists posit that the Anunnaki may have had a direct hand in the construction of these structures, using their advanced technology and knowledge to engineer some of the most impressive and perplexing ancient feats of architecture.Chapter 3 delves into the contemporary theories and potential sightings of the Anunnaki in the modern world, leading us to ponder the possibility that they could still exist in some capacity, whether on earth or in another dimension. This chapter raises questions about unexplained phenomena, such as alien sightings, UFO sightings, and so-called "ancient astronaut theories". By exploring these ideas, we open the door to a world beyond our own, where ancient beings and beings from another planet have a piece of the puzzle in human history.Chapter 4 takes us even deeper into the mythology and legend that surrounds the Anunnaki, exploring the many tales and stories that have been passed down from generation to generation throughout history. It examines how these stories have been used to create cultural and religious identities, giving way to unique belief systems such as Hinduism, Shintoism, and Greek mythology, to name just a few. By examining the broader impact of the Anunnaki on human civilization, we see that their influence extends far beyond ancient Sumeria, reaching into the very fabric of world culture today.Finally, Chapter 5 concludes with a reflection on the significance of the Anunnaki in human history, whether they existed in the documented sense, or not. By exploring the Anunnaki's story, we gain a unique insight into the mysterious and often inexplicable beginnings of human civilization, sparking a renewed sense of wonder and curiosity about the great mysteries of the universe. As such, the Anunnaki has proven to be a timeless subject, inspiring and intriguing scholars, theorists, and the general populace for centuries; their impact and influence continue to be felt throughout our global community even to this day.

Chapter 6

The Anunnaki's SideSynopsis: The Anunnaki, an ancient race of extraterrestrial beings, have lived among us on Earth for centuries, unbeknownst to humanity. They have always kept to themselves, watching from afar as humanity grew and developed into the civilization we are today.But when a group of humans stumble upon an Anunnaki artifact, the Anunnaki's cover is blown, and they must choose between revealing themselves to the world or retreating back into the shadows.As the Anunnaki tell their side of the story, the reader is taken on a journey through history as they reveal the role they played in humanity's development, including the creation of the very first humans. They explain their ethics, beliefs, and motivations, as well as the dark side of their power. As they weigh their options, both humanity and the Anunnaki face a crossroads that could forever change the course of history.The book culminates in an epic conflict between the Anunnaki and those who would seek to exploit their secrets, forcing both sides to confront the consequences of their actions and change the course of their respective futures.Throughout the journey, the Anunnaki provide a unique perspective on the meaning of existence, the power of the universe, and the cross-section between spirituality and science. At its core, this book is a story of identity, purpose, and the search for truth in a world shrouded in mystery.

Chapter 7

Unveiling the Anunnaki's Role in Humanity's Development In the dim past, before humanity's recorded history, the Anunnaki had descended on earth. They were an otherworldly race of beings, vastly superior to any living creature on the planet. For centuries, the Anunnaki observed human development from afar, playing an unseen yet vital role in humankind's evolution and progress.The Anunnaki's perspective was unique, and their knowledge of the universe and its workings were unparalleled to any humans who ever lived. They had a grand purpose, to guide humanity and help them understand their place in the cosmic order of things. They started by creating Homo sapiens, humans as we know them.The process of creating humanity was a complex one, requiring careful attention and precise genetic engineering. The Anunnaki infused their own DNA with that of early hominids to create a being that would be capable of higher consciousness and awareness. But as with any scientific endeavor, there were complications and consequences that would arise from creating a new species.One of the most significant dilemmas faced by the Anunnaki was their desire to deliver knowledge and wisdom to humans. While their intentions were undoubtedly noble, their power was so vast that their influence could lead humanity down the wrong path. They were, after all, alien beings who had their own ideas and value systems. Thus, the Anunnaki had to carefully choose what they imparted to humanity and what they kept hidden.Over the course of human history, the Anunnaki watched and guided humanity as it progressed from stone-age societies to the current modern-day civilization that we know. They directed humanity's intellectual and spiritual development, bringing forth revolutionary concepts and inventions that humans could never have achieved on their own.Yet, despite their influence, the Anunnaki remained a shadowy and mysterious presence, scarcely mentioned in the annals of history. Even though myths and legends referred to them, it was always as a distant and god-like entity that remained unapproachable and out of reach.That all changed when a group of humans discovered an Anunnaki artifact that turned out to be a game-changer. Suddenly, humanity found out about the Anunnaki's existence, creating a dilemma for the Alien beings as they had always remained in the shadows. The Anunnaki were now forced to divulge their origin and purpose, revealing their role in human history, and confront the moral dilemmas and ethical issues that emerged with their involvement in human development.

Chapter 8

The Anunnaki's EthosAs the Anunnaki grapple with the sudden exposure of their existence, they take the opportunity to open up about their beliefs and motivations. They reveal a culture shaped by a deep sense of responsibility towards the development of civilization on earth. In the Anunnaki's eyes, they are caretakers and stewards tasked with nurturing the growth of humanity and guiding it towards universal harmony.They explain that their ethos is built on three core principles: knowledge, wisdom, and balance.Knowledge, to the Anunnaki, was not just information but insights and understanding of the universe's workings. They believe that knowledge must be sought relentlessly and disseminated to all those who seek it. According to the Anunnaki, the highest form of knowledge is self-knowledge, understanding the true nature of one's being.Wisdom, on the other hand, was the ability to apply knowledge effectively. Wisdom, in the Anunnaki's eyes, is the finely-honed ability to navigate life's complexities to achieve a better understanding of oneself and the world. Balance was the final cornerstone of their ethos, and perhaps the most critical. They understand that power unchecked leads to corruption and ruin, and thus view temperance and harmony as essential to life's journey. The

Anunnaki's role, in this regard, is to preserve balance, a delicate balance between light and dark, good and evil.Their ethos is grounded in this tri-fold belief, and it shapes their entire decision-making process. The Anunnaki felt a great sense of responsibility for the decisions they made as they recognized the immense power they wielded. It was this ethos that guided their decision-making as they considered whether to reveal themselves to humanity or retreat back into the shadows.As they explored the dark side of their power and the unintended consequences of their actions, the Anunnaki acknowledged their shortcomings. They recognized the need to assess their influence critically. The profound responsibility they felt to guide humanity could, when unchecked, lead to a moral dilemma, and ethical complexity would emerge. This deep contemplation sharpened the Anunnaki's introspection, leading them to challenge themselves continually. The Anunnaki's ethos is a potent mix of knowledge, wisdom, and balance, one that beautifully intertwines spirituality and science. The guiding principles have seen the Anunnaki shape the development of human civilization and culture, and the resulting consequences, both intended and unintended, have influenced how they continue to nurture human growth to this day.

Chapter 9

A Clash of Worlds As the Anunnaki deliberated whether to reveal themselves to humanity or retreat back into the shadows, they became painfully aware of the dangers that lay ahead. The human world was not ready to receive their knowledge and power, and the Anunnaki feared it would be exploited for personal gain. They were equally worried about the moral and ethical implications of their power. They knew that their decision would have consequences that could affect the course of history.Sadly, these fears were not unfounded. There were those who weaponized the Anunnaki's knowledge, using it for their own agendas, causing a significant rift between the two worlds. Those in power, both human and non-human, felt threatened by the Anunnaki's potential to challenge their authority and control. They saw the Anunnaki as nothing more than a means to an end, to be used as tools for their own gain, and had little respect for their ancient culture and beliefs.The situation became increasingly tense, eventually leading to an all-out conflict between the two worlds. As the Anunnaki prepared to defend their values and beliefs, they knew that they could no longer remain passive. They needed to take a stand to protect their heritage and the human beings they had helped create.The battle that ensued was not just a physical clash, but a moral and ethical one, testing the Anunnaki's ethos to the limit. The

Anunnaki took up arms and entered the fray, determined to preserve their legacy and defend humanity's interest. They realized that their intervention had been critical to human civilization, helping it evolve and progress in ways that would not have been possible without their guidance.As for the humans fighting with the Anunnaki, they were initially apprehensive. Humanity had always been skeptical of the otherworldly beings, and the revelation of their existence had created a wave of uncertainty and fear. But as the conflict continued, the humans fighting alongside the Anunnaki began to understand the true significance of the beings they shared the battlefield with. They saw the Anunnaki's ethos at work and understood that their values aligned with humanity's own aspirations for peace and harmony.Despite the challenges, the Anunnaki continued to fight on, overcoming their opponents and solidifying their commitment to mankind. In the end, they triumphed, but the victory didn't come without a price. The sacrifice the Anunnaki made during this battle had a profound impact on them, changing their outlook, and ultimately leading to their departure from Earth.The conflict between the Anunnaki and humanity revealed much of what defines both cultures. Yet, it was the Anunnaki's ethos of knowledge, wisdom, and balance that truly proved essential in guiding their decision-making and guiding humanity towards peace, progress, and harmony. As for the human race, it was a stark reminder that the Anunnaki's power and influence were not to be taken lightly and were critical in shaping human civilization.

Chapter 10

From the Anunnaki perspective, Earth would have appeared like a primitive and young planet, lacking much of the advanced technology and knowledge that their civilization had developed. When we first visited Earth, we were struck by the vast potential of the planet and its inhabitants. We saw that humans had the potential to become a sophisticated species, but they needed guidance and help to do so.Our civilization had already advanced beyond the wildest dreams of humans. We had mastered interstellar travel, genetic engineering, metallurgy, and astronomy. We hoped to share some of our knowledge and technology with humans to give them a chance to evolve and grow as a civilization.We viewed ourselves as the merchants of knowledge and wisdom. We had a duty to ensure that lesser species, such as humans, had the tools necessary to advance and survive. We taught them valuable skills such as agriculture, architecture, mathematics, and science. Over time, we watched as humans transformed from hunter-gatherers to farmers and builders.Our influence on Earth can be seen in the mythology and beliefs of ancient cultures. We were revered as gods who controlled the fate of humanity. Our creations, such as the pyramids in Egypt and the ziggurats in Mesopotamia, stand as testaments to the knowledge and technologies we shared with humans.Although our time on Earth was limited, we left behind a legacy that would impact the planet for centuries to come. We continue to be fascinated by the humans' progress and their ability to use the knowledge and technologies we shared with them in new and innovative ways.As the Anunnaki civilization, we were honored to have played a role in the evolution of humans and the transformation of the planet. We will always be grateful for our time on Earth and the opportunity to share our wisdom and knowledge with such a remarkable species.